Dad

Father, Friend & Hero

Flairs and Glairs

Publication House

"Dad- Father, Friend & Hero"

ISBN No: "978-93-90799-56-5"
1st Edition
Language – English and Hindi

Flairs and Glairs
Publication House
Regd. Under MSME Act.

Disclaimer

This is a work of fiction and solely represent the thoughts of the corresponding authors of the articles. Our editors have tried their best to edit the content of all the authors and check the plagiarism.
All the write-ups in this book are unique and are only published in this book.
In case any plagiarism or error is found, only the author is responsible alone, and not the publisher or the Compilers.

Cover Designing and Book Formatting
Shubham Shah

Acknowledgement

I would like to express my special thanks of gratitude to all my co-authors and team members who helped me to publish this Anthology. Without your Hardwork, Love and Support, it would not be possible to publish the book.

We are thankful Flairs and Glairs Publication, without whom, this projectwould never have been possible. Moreover a special thanks to our beloved parents, relatives and friends for their continuous support and encouragement towards us in completing this book.

Once again Thanks to all my Co-authors for being a part of this Anthology and also for believing and helping me to publish this Anthology.

Co Author

Shubham Shah (Founder Flairs and Glairs)
Ishani Agarwal (Co-Founder Flairs and Glairs)

1. Aman Sharma (Compiler)
2. Shree Ram Pandey
3. Shalini Soumya
4. Ruchi Rani
5. Bhavana Manani
6. Sahina Ghugha
7. Nikita Gajraj
8. Aastha Gulati
9. Aditya Srivastava
10. Ratnesh Paras Singh
11. Ishrat Jahan Noormohammed Khan
12. Pragya Verma
13. Kritika Mehta
14. Darshankumar Dilipbhai Patel
15. Deepshikha Nathawat
16. Sakshi Jain
17. Vidisha Agarwal
18. Raghuveer
19. Sakshi Jain
20. Bhavna Kumari
21. Shazia Jabeen
22. Vaibhav Gupta
23. Devendra Dhakad
24. Ashis Pahi
25. Smita Kumari
26. Ankita Sahoo
27. Niraj Yadav
28. Kalamkaar
29. Jeevitha.S
30. Harshita Verma

31. Shubhashish Ranjan
32. Krishna Motwani
33. Padma Srivastava
34. Hema Kirthiga J
35. Jayashree Sahoo
36. Shivani Singh
37. Devyani Neral
38. Drishti Bai
39. Bilal Khan
40. Sayak Ghosh
41. Udayan Chetia
42. Kareena Verma
43. Debesh Prusty
44. Pragyan Panda
45. Priyanka Varma
46. Nivetha R C
47. Prangya Pramita Sahu
48. Mohanapriya.K
49. Shradha Gindlani
50. Shadma Ali
51. Ankita Bhatia

Shubham Shah

(Founder- Flairs and Glairs)

Shubham Shah, an entrepreneur at "Flairs & Glairs" a brand with dynamics in events organizing and cultural educational pan INDIA, is a 26yrs old guy who recently has entered the digital platform of imprinting emotions. He has initiated with his own open mic platform to help budding poets and aspiring writers under his brand named as "Teekhe Zasbaaat"

He is a commerce graduate from the Bhagalpur City of Bihar.
He states Writing has impersonated him since childhood and he has now been writing for over a decade!
Cooking, on the other hand, is his passion! He also mentions, trying out new things just tickles him!
When asked sir, Why SPICY EMOTIONS?
He smiled and added, “agar jasbaat teekhe na ho toh wo jasbaat kahan” Spices are all that blends! So do his words!
As a chef, he presents to you his dish! Hot and freshly served! Taste it! Feel it! Enjoy it! You can also find his writing in the Book “Teekhe Zasbaaat” and 50+ Co-authored anthologies. With his passion to explore opportunities across Platforms, he is working with keen devotion and We wish him all the very best for his future ventures.
He is Featured in the **International Magazine De-Mode** for his upcoming solo novel.
He is **Approved by Ne8x for its Lit Fest,** and is a **Golden Star Awards 2020 Winner.**
He is an **India Book of Records Holder** for his Anthology **Satrang,** and has the **Grandmaster** title by **Asia Book of Records**, for the same.
He has also been featured in **Prabhat Khabar**, **Dainik Jagran** and other renowned Newspaper for his achievements.
He has also been awarded with **India Star Republic Award 2021.**
He has been a proud co-author to
India Book of Records (Title- Black)
World Book of Records (Title -15 Wonders of Poetries)
India Book of Records (Title - Aaina)
Vajra World Records Holder (Title - Gustakhi Maaf Hai)
High Range of Records Holder (Title - Gustakhi Maaf Hai)

Share your reviews on his

INSTAGRAM

@spicy_emotions
@shubham4shah

Or via email on

shubham2shah@gmail.com

To stay tuned to his work and opportunities follow his business Handles

INSTAGRAM FACEBOOK YOUTUBE

@flairsandglairs
@teekhezasbaaat

WEBSITE:

https://flairsandglairs.in/
https://flairsandglairs.com/

Ishani Agarwal

(Co-Founder- Flairs and Glairs)

Ishani Agarwal hails from the City of Joy, Kolkata.
She is the co-founder of her Community "Teekhe Zasbaat" and Flairs and Glairs Publication.
Been a Compiler for 45+ Anthologies, she is in the process for more. Co-authored in 150+ Anthologies. She is a India Book of Records Holder, a Vajra World Records Holder, a High Range of Records Holder and a Bravo Record holder.

Approved by Ne8x for its Lit Fest 2020, and Literary Icon 2020. Also a Golden Star Awards Winner 2020.
She has also been awarded with India Star Republic Award 2021.
She has been featured by the National Magazine "Taree Zameen Par" with the title 'unstoppable'.
Also featured in the International Magazine DeMode for her upcoming solo novel, she is proud to write on social issues, and is happy with the love she is receiving.
Connect with her on Instagram: @Ishani_agarwal_quotes / @compilations_so_far

COMPILER

Aman Sharma

Aman Sharma is currently pursuing his Bachelor's in Maths Honours but he is most interested in expressing his thoughts through his writings. Having a very intellectual mind which has a deep desire to explore the truth and causes of life and it's dilemma. He has already compiled 2 books- "Wo MAA hi to hai" and "Love yourself: Finding your Self-worth" and again he is also a co-author in about 15 anthologies.

YourQuote: http://www.yourquote.in/aman_gaurav

IG: @aman_shaan

अब समझ आता है

थका हुआ हूँ सफ़र का तो अब समझ आता है
तेरी खामोशी महज़ खामोशी नही थी; अब सैलाब नज़र आता है

हर कही गयी बातों का अब मतलब समझ आता है
तेरी हक़ीक़त कुछ और थी वो तनाव अब नज़र आता है

परदा कर रखा था मैंने जमाने की मुसीबतों का
क्यों हाथ थामा करता था तू अब समझ आता है

मैं नादान था तब कुछ समझ नही पाता था
तेरा झूठ के पीछे दर्द भरा सच छुपा लेना अब समझ आता है

कोसा करता था छोटी-छोटी बातों को लेकर जाने-अनजाने में
तू सहकर सबकुछ मुझे दिया तेरा प्यार नज़र आता है

ग़लत जो हुआ करता था कभी तेरा डर रहता था
मग़र वो तेरा फक्र से बेटा कहने वाला गर्व नजर आता है

बड़ा हुआ तो लगा जैसे तुझसे आगे बढ़ गया मैं
मग़र तू तबसे अब तक बाप ही था, अब समझ आता है

मैं बन नही सकता तुझ जैसा; काबिल नही समझता
अब जो तुझे समझ गया हूँ तो रब नजर आता है

थका हुआ हूँ सफ़र का तो अब समझ आता है
तेरी खामोशी महज़ खामोशी नही थी अब सैलाब नज़र आता है

श्री राम पाण्डेय

श्री राम पाण्डेय एक विद्यार्थी होने के साथ एक सुलझे व्यक्ति भी है। जितनी ताकत इनके मुस्कान में है, उतनी ही इनके कलम से पिरोएं शब्दो में झलकता है। आप सोच रहे होंगे वो कैसे, तो यूँ समझ लीजिए की दोनों कातिलाना है। हँस के भी आप के दिल को घायल कर सकते और अपने शब्दों से भी।

पापा-आप

धरती पे ईश्वर का रूप हो पापा-आप।
मेरे जीवन का शून्य से अनंत हो पापा-आप।।
कोई भी उलझन में राह दिखाते हो पापा-आप।
मुश्किल से लड़ना सिखाते हो पापा-आप।।
अंधियार में देकर साथ हौसला बढ़ाते हो पापा-आप।
दुनिया के इस भीड़ में उँगली पकड़ चलना सिखाते हो पापा-आप।।
अपने कंधे पे बैठा दुनिया दिखते हो पापा-आप।
दर्द को छिपा हमेशा मुस्कुराते हो पापा-आप।।
मुझे जानती दुनिया जिस नाम से वो पहचान हो पापा-आप।
मेरे जीवन का आधार हो पापा-आप।।
हूँ मैं आप का कृति।
इस पर अभिमान है मुझे।।

शालिनी सौम्या

शालिनी सौम्या अपने नाम के भांति सुंदर, शालिन और व्यवहार कुशल व्यक्तित्व है| कहने को तो अभी ये ग्यारहवीं की ही छात्रा है पर इनके हुनर आसमान सा ऊँचा है| एक बेहद हसमुख और मनमौजी लडक़ी! जिसकी मुस्कुराहट कामयाबी को छूने को बेताब है और बस वो उस मुस्कान से अपने माँ का नाम अपने से ऊँचा देखना चाहती है| माँ के प्रति लगाव उनका आशीर्वाद और शालिनी की लगन इन्हें जरूर एक दिन ऊंचा मकाम देगी|

पापा

नन्ही आँखे मेरी और मुड़ी हुई उंगलिया थी,
ये बात तब की है जब मेरी दुनिया आपकी छाँव थी |

तेरी छाँव लगा मुझे ये सब कुछ जैसे कुछ भी न था,
किसे पता था तब इन सब के पीछे जुनून किसका था ||

हर चीज़ माँगी हुई समय से पहले मिल जाती थी,
अब याद आता है तुमने छिपाई कितनी परेशानी थी |

एहसास न होने दिया किसी पल अपने जिम्मेदारियों का,
इतना साथ दिया कि अब मुझे डर ना रहा अंधेरो का ||

छिपा लो जितने भी गम मैं सब कुछ समझ सकती हूँ,
कैसे ना समझू पापा मैं तो आपकी ही लाडली बेटी हूँ !

कमी ना रही तब से अब तक मुझे किसी चीज़ की
कदर है मुझे बहोत आपके जिम्मेदारियों की !!

रुची रानी

रुची रानी स्नातकीय छात्रा हैं| इन्हें लिखने की कला और प्रेरणा हमारे प्रिय आदरणीय राष्ट्रकवि रामधारी सिंह "दिनकर" जी से मिली और ये भी यही चाहती हैं कि अपने लेखन से सबको ओत प्रोत कर सकें|

मेरे पापा

मेरी ताकत मेरी पूँजी
मेरी पहचान हैं मेरे पापा।
मेरी प्रेरणा मेरा आदर्श
मेरा अभिमान हैं मेरे पापा।।
मेरी सभी गलतियों को
सरलता से लेते हैं मेरे पापा।
विनम्रता से मेरी सभी गलतियों का
एहसास कराते हैं मेरे पापा।।
बड़ों का आदर और सम्मान करना
सिखाते हैं मेरे पापा।
ज़िन्दगी का असली मतलब
समझाते हैं मेरे पापा।।
मेरी हर एक इच्छा बिना कहे
जान लेते हैं मेरे पापा।
नासमझ हूँ फिर भी मेरी हर बात
मान लेते हैं मेरे पापा।।
मेरे सपनों को अपना सपना
बनाते हैं मेरे पापा।
सपने को पूरा करने का रास्ता
बताते हैं मेरे पापा।।
मुश्किल कि घड़ियों में
अक्सर साथ खड़े होते हैं मेरे पापा।
मेरी गलतियाँ होने पर भी
मेरे खातिर लड़ते हैं मेरे पापा।।
कड़ी मेहनत और ईमानदारी का
पाठ पढ़ाते हैं मेरे पापा।
इस स्वार्थी दुनिया में भी दूसरों की मदद
करना सिखाते हैं मेरे पापा।।
जीवन में समय का मूल्य

बताते हैं मेरे पापा।
सब के ऊपर प्यार और स्नेह
बरसाते हैं मेरे पापा।।
मेरे मार्गदर्शक मेरे पक्के दोस्त
और सच्चे हीरो हैं मेरे पापा।
मुझको हिम्मत देने वाले
मेरे स्वाभिमान हैं मेरे पापा।।
शायद रब ने देकर भेजा
फल ये अच्छे कर्मों का।
उसकी रहमत, करुणा, दया और
उसके वरदान हैं मेरे पापा।।

भावना मनानी

भावना मनानी उस्मानिया विश्वविद्यालय, हैदराबाद से वाणिज्य (कॉमर्स) में स्नातक की उपाधि प्राप्त कर रही है। अपने शिक्षाविदों के अलावा, वह लेखन में भी पाई जाती हैं। "लेखन केवल एक कला नहीं है, यह आत्मा की संतुष्टि है। लेखन एक भावना है जिसे केवल कुछ ही महसूस कर सकते हैं!" ऐसा उनका मानना है। उनका समर्पण ही उन्हें किसी और से अलग करता है।

Your quote: https://www.yourquote.in/manani

कहते हैं, भगवान बेटियां हर किसी को नहीं देता है
क्युकी राजकुमारी को पलने की क्षमता
सिर्फ एक राजा ही रख सकता है!

मेरे प्यारे पापा!
मैं जानती हूँ पापा,
की आप मुझे कितना प्यार करते हो !

मेरी हर छोटी ख्वाईश को
पूरा करते हो आप!
मेरी हर जिद्द को कभी मना नहीं करते
क्युकी मे जानती हूँ पापा
की आप मुझे कितना प्यार करते हो !

मेरी नादानियों को भी झेलते हो
मेरी हर जिद्द पूरी करते हो
मेरी गलतियों को माफ़ करते हो
क्युकी मे जानती हूँ पापा
की आप मुझे कितना प्यार करते हो !

मेरी खुशियों की चाबी हो आप
मेरे चेहरे की मुस्कान हो आप
मेरे दिल का गुरुर हो आप
मेरे पहले गुरु भी आप ही तो हो !

बचपन मे चलना सिखाया,
सपनो को पूरा करने का हौसला
मेहनत का फल और
जिंदगी जीने का सलीका
सब आप ही से तो सीखा है मैंने!

मैं समझती हूँ, आसान नहीं होता
लड़कियों को आजादी देना,
फिर भी दुनिया की न सोच
मुझे जिंदगी जीने का मौका दिया आपने!
क्युकी मे जानती हूँ पापा
की आप मुझे कितना प्यार करते हो !
आपका ये विश्वास मैं कभी टूटने नहीं दूंगी पापा!

आप ही मेरे हीरो हो
मेरे लिए सब कुछ हो आप!
आपकी दौलत नहीं चाहिए
मेरे लिए तो आपका साया ही काफी है!

आपकी बेटी
भावना!

Sahina Ghugha

.

Sahina Ghugha is 20 year old B.Com student at Saurashtra University Rajkot. She is state level winner in poetry competition 2017. She is Co-author of 10+ anthologies. She is an amazing writer and poet and she wants do something for society through her pen.
Insta ID- Itz_Sahina_write

<u>पिता एक चाह है</u>

पिता एक चाह है, पिता मंज़िल तक पहोचती राह है।
पिता जीत का जुनून है, पिता रगो में दौड़ता खून है।

पिता एक उसूल है, पिता संस्कारो का मूल है।
पिता गर्व और शान है, पिता ईश्वर पे रहा इमान है।

पिता एक उम्मीद है, पिता पूरी करता हर ज़िद है।
पिता देखता बच्चो का फायदा है, पिता कानून और कायदा है।

पिता एक अच्छा राग है, पिता अच्छा वाला दाग है।
पिता पैसों का हिसाब है, पिता बच्चे का ख़्वाब है।

पिता एक वरदान है, पिता से ही होती पहेचान है।
पिता बहेती सरिता है, पिता "साहिना" की कविता हैं।

निकिता गजराज

निकिता गजराज
MA economics
हंसमुख स्वभाव की धनी, समाजसेवी व्यवहार
अपने विचारों को बिना हिचकिचाहट बिना डरे सबके सामने रखने वाली

मेरा साहस मेरी इज़्ज़त

मेरा सम्मान है मेरे पापा
मेरी ताकत मेरी पूंजी...
मेरी पहचान है मेरे पापा....!!
घर की एक एक ईट में...
शामिल उनका खून पसीना ...
सारे घर की रौनक उनसे..
सारे घर की शान है मेरे पापा !!
मेरी इज़्ज़त मेरी शौहरत...
मेरा रुतबा मेरा मान है मेरे पापा...
मुझे हिम्मत देने वाला
मेरा अभिमान है मेरे पापा....!!
सारे रिश्ते उनके दम से
सारी बाते उनसे है.....
सारे घर के दिल की धड़कन
सारे घर की जान है मेरे पापा..!!
शायद रब ने देकर भेजा फल ये अच्छे कर्मो का .....
उसकी रहमत उसकी नियामत
उसका है वरदान मेरे पापा...

Aastha Gulati

आस्था गुलाटी स्वर्गीय श्री राजेश कुमार की सुपुत्री है।उनकी माता श्रीमती रजनी वाणिज्य की अध्यापिका है।उनका जन्म 12 अप्रैल 2004 पानीपत में हुआ था। उन्होंने दसवीं की परीक्षा सीबीएसई बोर्ड से करी है। उनकी रूचि लिखने व नृत्य पर है। उन्होंने ये कविता अपने स्वर्गीय पिता की याद मै लिखी है।

याद आपकी आती है!!

पापा हर बात पर याद आपकी आती है,
पापा हर बात पर याद आपकी सताती है।
कोई अ से आप कहे, या ब से बाप,
कोई च चाय कहे, या ड से डाट,
पापा हर बात पर याद आपकी आती है।

पापा याद आपकी आती है जब करे कोई जिक्र प्यार का
क्योंकि सच्ची मोहब्बत तो आप ही अपनी बेटी से करते थे ना,
पापा याद आपकी सताती है जब पुकारे कोई नाम मेरा।

पापा आपकी इकलौती बेटी थी मै,
हां मै जानती हूं आपको फक्र था इस बात पे,
पर नाजने क्यों दुनिया को ये अनिष्ट सा लगता है।
पापा आपके जाने के बाद पता लगा मुझे मेरी तो पूरी दुनिया ही आप थे,
अब तो यह दुनिया बस आंखें दिखाना जानती है,
बस आंखें दिखाना जानती है।

पहले तो डर कभी लगा नहीं क्योंकि विश्वास था
आप हो ना पर अब हर वक्त एक डर सताता है,
पर अब हर वक्त एक डर सताता है।
पापा आज पता लगा मुझे बाप क्या कहलाता है।
ज्यादा तो नहीं पर जितना वक्त आपने मेरे साथ बिताया उसी वक्त में सब सीखला दिया।

सिखलाया आपने कैसे खुद के लिए लड़ना है,
सिखलाया आपने कैसे मां का ध्यान रखना है,
सिखलाया आपने खुद ही पर विश्वास करना है,

सिखलाया आपने ही इस दुनिया में खड़ा रहना।
आपकी सिखाई हर बात याद है मुझे और यह भी याद है कितने प्यार से आप सिखाते थे मुझे।

पापा हर बात पे याद आपकी आती है,
पापा हर बात पे याद आपकी सताती है।
कोई ई से ईमान कहे, या फ से फरियाद,
कोई ग से गुस्सा कहे, या ह से हिम्मत
पापा हर बात पे याद आपकी आती है,
पापा हर बात पे याद आपकी सताती है,
हर बात पे याद आपकी सताती है।

Aditya Srivastava

I am Aditya Srivastava from Uttar Pradesh.
Working in Sanjay Gandhi Post Graduate Institute of Medical Sciences (SGPGIMS LUCKNOW)
Email.id- srivastavaaditya515@gmail.com.

पापा

पापा जब हम इस शब्द को सुनते हैं तो लगता है की जीवन की हर खुशियां हमारे पास है।
जब भी उन्हें कोई भी चीज अच्छी लगती है तो वो खुद से ज्यादा हमारे लिए करते है।

खुद कितना बड़ा ही कारण हो कभी भी सामने उन्हें रोता हुआ नही देखा।
हर एक गम को सीने में छिपा कर अकेले एक बंद कमरे में रोता हुआ देखा है मैंने।

कौन कहता है कि बाप होना आसान है,
जिस प्रकार माँ अपने बच्चे को सीने से लगा कर रखती है ,
तो बाप उनपर आने वाली हर एक मुशीबत को रोकता है,
पापा से अच्छा कोई दोस्त नही होता,
पापा से अच्छा कोई प्यार नही होता ,
कद्र करना अपने माँ बाप का जीवन भर ,
क्योंकि ये वही प्यार है जिसमे धोखा नही होता।।।

रत्नेश पारस सिंह

मेरा नाम रत्नेश पारस सिंह है। मेरा जन्म U.P में हुआ था 1/11/1999 को। मैं एक सकारात्मक व्यक्ति हूं और मैंने पापा पर कुछ पंक्तियां लिखी हैं आशा करता हुँ की आप सभी को पसंद आएगा।

मैं पेशे से कराटे कोच और अंतरराष्ट्रीय खिलाड़ी हूं। मैं कुछ अलग करने की सोच रखता हुँ और अपने पूरे परिवार के साथ एक स्वस्थ और खुशहाल जीवन जीना चाहता हूं।

पिता के रुप मे है.....भगवान

पापा तो हमारे ख्वाहिशो के भंडार होते है |
जिस चिज की ख्वाहिश करते हम उसे हमारे सामने रख देते है ||
जो कडी़ मेहनत दिन रात एक कर दे तुम्हारे लिए |
उसे संसार मे पिता के रुप मे भगवान कहते है ||

पापा कभी गुस्सा करते तो कभी कायनात का प्यार तुम्हे देते |
तुम्हे देखकर हर सुबह घर से निकल जाते ||
वो अपनी खुशीयो की ऊचाई देखते है तुम्हारे अंदर |
जब घर आते है तो वो तुम्हे हस्ता हुआ देख मुस्कुरा जाते |

मुश्किल समय में भी तुम्हारा साथ दे वो पापा होते है |
तुमसे दुर रहकर भी तुम्हारे पास रहे वो पापा होते है||
जब भी हमे किसी चिज की जरुरत पड़े |
अपना हर एक लहु बहा के तुम्हे हंसाने वाले पापा होते है ||

हमारी जरुरते पुरा करने के लिए सुरज से पहले जाग, घर से निकल जाते है |
हमारे लिए पापा कडी़ धुप मै और काटों पे भी चल जाते है |
हम जब जिद्द करते है, पैसे की तो वो हमे पॉकेट मनी देते है
हमारा भविष्य बनाने के लिए वो हद से गुजर जाते है ||

पापा मेहनत करके हमारी जिंदगी मे रोज दिवाली मनाते है
तुम्हे नए-नए कपड़े देते तुम्हारी जिंदगी के हर पल को सजाते है ||
जो खुद के लिए जल्दी कपड़े ना खरीद सके |
वो पापा हमारी सारी मन्नते पुरी करते है ||

पिता को पाया है भगवान के रुप मे |
माथा टेकु मै उनके सामने हर सुख-दुख मे ||

खुद जो तुम्हारे दुख का हिस्सेदार बन जाए।
उनके सामने भगवान भी माथा टेके हर पल में।।

भगवान कभी दुर ना करना मेरे पापा को मेरी जिंदगी से।
उनकी उम्र बढ़ा देना मेरी जिंदगी से।।
मै हर पल मे तेरा गुलाम बन जाऊँगा मेरे खुदा।
कभी ये प्यार का डोर ना तोड़ना हमारी खुशहाल भरी जिंदगी से।।

Ishrat Jahan Noormohammed Khan

Ms Ishrat jahan khan is a passionate Teacher and a Writer she loves reading and writing. Loving and caring is her hobby. And keep learning and accept the positive suggestion is her quality.She belongs to North India and stays at Ulhasnagar (Maharashtra).
Loves humanity always.

पापा

पापा मेरी जान है
वो मेरा अरमान है
मेरी मुस्कान है
वो ही मेरी पहचान है

हसना उन्होनो सिखाया
चलना उन्होंने सिखाया
जिंदगी जीना सिखाया
गलत से दूर रहना सिखाया

जिंदगी की डोर
जिंदगी की हर छोर
बस पापा आप हो
हर वजह जीने की आप हो...

You are hero

Papa you are my hero
Without you I am zero
You are my lifeline
Which always shine

You are my inspiration
You are my destination
You are my motivation
You are my highest designation

You always make me bold
When I am stresses you hold
You make me proud
You are never shroud.....

Pragya Verma

Pragya Verma hails from Prayagraj, Uttar Pradesh. She is a poetess and a writer. She has done 78+ anthologies, and two international anthologies and currently doing two world record anthologies as a co-author. She is also compiling two anthologies named, "SHADES OF NIGHT", "In a Relationship with Success". She has a great interest in making paintings and doing photography. She loves to gain spiritual knowledge and tries to find peace everywhere. You can follow her on Instagram: @wordsofpragya

My Hero

You are my hero dad,
You never let me to be sad.

Your face is something I want to see everyday,
You have made my life like a fairytale.

Always fulfilled my all wishes,
With you my life is full of blisses.

Yes! You are my crazy friend,
With whom craziness never end.

I and mom love you so much,
I know I had never said this much.

You are my first love,
When you smile you shine like a stars above.

Dad! You are my everything,
Without you, I'm nothing.

कृतिका मेहता

इनका नाम कृतिका मेहता है. ये जयपुर की रहने वाली हैं और ये एक साधारण सी लेखिका जिन्हें उध्दरणउल्लेख के साथ-साथ संगीत में भी रूची हैं,
ये अपने लेख प्रतिदिन इंस्टाग्राम पेज पर पोस्ट करती हैं, कृप्या आप अपने समय अनुकूल इनके लेख को पढने के लिए और इनके लेख पर अपनी राय comment द्वारा देने के लिए इन्हें इंस्टाग्रगाम पर फालो कर सकते हैं, इनका इंस्टाग्राम पेज हैं-@freelywriting14

ऐसा मेरे पापा का प्यार

लब पर दुआओं सा,
आँखो मे नमी सा,
और दुखों में होठों की खुशी सा,
जिसकी दुआओं में पलता मेरा संसार,
ऐसा मेरे पापा का प्यार।

Darshankumar Dilipbhai Patel

Here by Darshan Patel physiotherapist,compiler from Nadiad, Gujarat ,co author who writes about life and with the aim to inspire a one and motivate to those who loose their hope in life and also about that fact of life. A true inspiration from chaanakya niti, bhagwat geeta, santram saurabh, social media, and learning lessons from ones life.
IG: @d.2p3

जी हाँ पापा!

नही है ,उनको पसीने की परवाह
परवाह है उन्हे एक छोटी सी मुस्कान की।
उंगली पकड़ के जिसने चलना सिखाया,
कंधो पे बिठा के जिसने जहाँ दिखाया।
घरको संभालने मे दीन रात लगा दिये,
घरके कुलदीपको के दिये जला दिये।
खुदकी बुझती जिंदगीको नज़रंदाज कर दिया
बच्चों की जिंदगीको सवार दिया।
हा पापा ,जिन्होंने कभी अपने आँशु छुपा लिए
महान ऐक्टर है पापा!
दिलपे पत्थर रखके चेहरे पे हँसी,
भिन्न भिन्न किरदार निभाये,
कभी दोस्त ,कभी शिक्षक, तो कभी माँ!
कभी भरोसा ,तो कभी होंसला।
हा पापा ,
जिन्होंने अपनो के लिए सब कुछ दाव पे लगा दीया,
जिंदगी की हर डगर पे सहारा दीया।
जो खुद टूट जाते है, बच्चों की इमारत बनाने मे।
पुरा दीन दुःख क्या, सुख क्या
शाम की हँसी का इंतज़ार किया।
खुद की खुशियों को ऐसे तैनात किया,
बच्चों की खुशियों को ही अपना मान लीया।
पाई पाई को जमा कर बड़ा किया,
कदम कदम चला कर खडा किया।
कभी कोई आँच नहीं आने दी,
आह! बोलते ही दोड लगा दी।
मुस्केलियो से लड के जिंदगीको जीना सिखाया,
कभी डरना नहीं, हिम्मत से चलना सिखाया।
शाम होते ही घरको बुलाया,
प्यार से सर पर हाथ रखके चैन की नींद सुलाया।

Deepshikha Nathawat

मेरा नाम दीपशिखा नाथावत है| मैं गुजरात के वडोदरा शहर में अपने बेटे के साथ रहती हूँ|मुझे बचपन से ही लिखने का शौक है|मैं जब 14 साल की थी तब से लिखना शुरू किया|मुझे लिखने के साथ साथ संगीत सुनने का और उसे गुनगुनाना बहुत अच्छा लगता है|मैं एक केमिकल कंपनी में कार्यालय सहायक के रूप में काम करती हूँ|

Dear पापा,
आपको खोया तो समझ आया कि क्या थे आप मेरे..
आप क्या गए इस जिंदगी से मुझे उम्र भर का गम दे गए..
जन्मदिन पर मेरे जब नींद में मिठाई खिलाते थे मुझे..
खत्म ना हो कभी वो बिखरता आंसुओं का मातम दे गए..
कैसे बंया करु में दिल का हाल आपको सब पता तो है
कैसे कहूँ कि सब ठीक है ना बीत पाए ऐसा मौसम दे गए..
आपके जाने के बाद कितना सताया इस दुनिया ने मुझे
आप थे तो सब था पास क्यों अकेलेपन का आलम दे गए..

कांधे पर बिठाकर मुझे झुला झुलाते थे वो,
थक जाती तो मुझे अपनी गोद मे सुलाते थे वो।
जिद्द करके अपनी हर बात मै उनसे मनवाती थी ,
जब कभी रूठ जाती तो मुझे प्यार से मनाते थे वो।
होती उदास जब भी तो मेरी उदासी भांप लेते थे वो,
मेरा ध्यान भटाकर मुझे उस उदासी से हटाते थे वो।
जब भी मेरी नादानीयों पर मुझे मेरी माँ डाँटती थी,
बडी चतुराई से मेरी माँ की डाँट से मुझे बचाते थे वो।
घर मे सबसे छोटी ,शैतान और बडी नटखट थी मैं,
कभी कभार गुस्से मे प्यार से मुझे चपत लगाते थे वो।
आज भी मेरे चेहरे और मेरे संस्कारो मे झलक है उनकी,
हर दर्द मे मरहम बनकर अपना अहसास दिलाते है वो।।

Sakshi Jain

Co-author Sakshi Jain is a good writer from Hathras
She has completed her diploma and currently pursuing B.Tech
She has been writing poetry from 1 year as her passion.
She wants to be a self publishing author in future.
Follow her writings on instagram: @_shenu_writings_

My hero

मैने पापा को मेरे जीवन में सूरज की जगमगाती किरण बनते हुए देखा है,

मैने पापा को चाँद सी चमकती चाँदनी बनते हुए देखा है,

मैने सबकी खुशी में पापा को अपने गम भुलाते हुए देखा है,

मैने सूरज को डूबते हुए देखा है
मौसमों को बदलते हुए देखा है,

मैने हर तकलीफ में पापा को मुस्कुराते हुए देखा है,
अपने सपने आधे छोड़ कर मेरे लिये LIC की किश्ते भरते हुए देखा है,

अपनी चोट भूल कर मेरे दर्द पर रोते हुए देखा है,

अँधेरे भरी इस दुनिया में मैने पापा को मेरे जीवन में उजाला बनते हुए देखा है,

मेरा हीरो और कोई नही है क्यूंकि मैने पापा को अपना सुपरहीरो बनते हुए देखा है।।

Vidisha Agarwal

She is an amazing writer, a passionate dancer and a very good cook.
IG: @vidiagr26

Pitaah!!

Kehte sunna hai maine
Baap beti ke rishte ke mayne...
Pita ki parchai hoti hai beti
Janam leti hai jab ek beti....
Pita roye do hi baar
Ek baar jab beti aaye
Ek baar jab beti jaaye...
Bass fark itna hai janaab
Ankh bharne ke mayne hai anjaan...
Log kehte hai beta dega budhe Maa Baap ka sath
Par Bass ek pita Kahe annt tak beti degi saath ...
Bhale hi ho jae Vo dusre ke ghar ki bahu
Lekin rahegi Sada Meri dil ki wohi tukdi..
Beti Kahe Khush rahe sada mere pitaah
Pitaah se hi naam
pitaah se hi h sansaar...

Rughveer

Rughveer is from Rajasthan.
IG: @rrughveerkumar

"मेरी कलम फीकी पड़ जाती है,
क्या लिखूं मैं उन के बारे में,
पिता से बढ़कर कोई नहीं ,
संसार सारे में"||

"बाहर कैसे रहता होगा बेटा,
यह चिंता उसे रोज सताती है |
कहीं मेरा बेटा भूखा ना रह जाए ,
यह कहकर एक रोटी ज्यादा खिलाती है,
दुनिया के सारे दर्द दूर हो जाते हैं, जब मां प्यार से मुझे सहलाती है"||

Sakshi Jain

She is Sakshi Jain from Roorkee, Uttarakhand. Pursuing B.A.Sociology.She is a social- worker and a decent girl.Her Instagram handle is @sakshijain_writes. She never quits in her life.

जब मैं सो रही थी,
कोई चुपके से सर पर हाथ फिरा रहा था
वह है पापा!
सपने तो मेरे थे उन्हें पूरा करने का रास्ता कोई और दिखा रहा था
वह है पापा!
मैं तो नौकरी के लिए घर से जाने पर दुखी थी , मुझसे भी अधिक आंसू कोई और बहा रहा था
वह है पापा!
जब मैं रो रही थी कोई चुपके से आया मुझे चुप कराया
वह है पापा !!
जब मैं जोर जोर से हंस रही थी कोई मेरे साथ ताल से ताल मिला रहा था वह है पापा !!
मुझे कोई और दुख नहीं सारे सुख दे रहा था वह है पापा!! मुझे कोई पीछे से गले लगा रहा था मुश्किलों में साथ दे रहा था वह है पापा !!
गुस्सा जब मैं थी कोई मुझे हंसा रहा था वह है पापा !!
शांति छवि और मोहनी मूरत है उन्हें उस इंसान की जो है मेरे पापा!!
कोई इंसान मेरे दिल में वास करने वाला है वह है पापा!!
कभी कोई मुश्किलों में साथ देने वाले वाले और कोई नहीं जब थे मेरे पापा!!
जो इंसान कह रहा था कि मैं चांद सितारे भी ले आऊंगा वह है पापा!!
आई लव यू पापा!

Bhavna kumari

She is a student....
And a dancer by passion.
She loves to dance and fond of music.

Dear papa,

You are my super hero,as well as a freind,who always supports me to move on the way I want to move on.you are the hero who can bring anything I want.you are the only one who can bring me a smile whenever I am sad .When ever I am sad you make me laugh and joke with you ,still why not you may be in difficulties. Your love and care to me is even more than god.you are the one who make me the happiest soul.whenever I want to fly you take me up in your arms and I really felt like to be flying.when I want to drive, you make me sit infront of you and I felt like driving.when I made the dish for the first time it was you who didn't tired of appreciating me.whenever mamma called me a 'junglee',it was you who replied her as making me ride on your back as I would be the queen of jungle.whenever you would miss me,you used to see my pics and kept it close to your heart.I am proud to call myself 'papa ki pari' and you 'my superhero'

Your fan
Your daughter,
Bhavna

Shazia Jabeen

Name: Shazia Jabeen
Parents: Abdul Hadi & Naziya Anjum
Studying: High School
Institute: Sri Chaitanya Techno Curriculum
Native place: Tandur, Vikarabad, District Telengana

Some people don't believe in heroes but they haven't met my dad." – ...

"My father gave me the greatest gift anyone could give another person, he believed in me." – ...

"A father is neither an anchor to hold us back nor a sail to take us there but a guiding light whose love shows us the way." –

It's a tall order being a perfect dad as kids want a male role model who is cool, calm and cuddly.

For a survey has revealed the qualities that make the ideal father figure include being seen as trendy, having plenty of patience but also dishing out hugs at home.

He must also spend more time with the family than his mates, treat mum with respect and be a safe driver.

According to a panel of 1,500 children aged six to 18-years-old, the number one feature of the best dad is one who makes them feel special and loved, with six in 10 putting it at the top of the list.

The ideal father figure should be seen as trendy, having plenty of patience but also dishing out hugs at home

My Daddy Strongest! He's also the wittiest, coolest and most loving! Yup, you don't really need reasons to prove that your Dad is super awesome. But if you ever did, then these 11 reasons will just make you go up to the man and give him a huge hug, not just on Fathers Day but every single day!

He taught us the important lesson of rising, falling and rising again.

He always taught us to work hard and inspired us to reach for the stars.

He showed us the world and its beauty on his shoulders – the safest place on earth

He taught us to appreciate the little joys of life

He let us believe that we were in the driver's seat on many of life's adventures

.He always took time out to make us feel special

He made us believe we could be whoever we wanted to be superhero child

He inspired us to be independent

Most importantly, he taught us how to love… unconditionally

Whenever required, he became our best friend.

Vaibhav Gupta

This is Vaibhav Gupta belonging to Kanpur, UP. He is a graduate and had worked in hospitality Field. He has keen interest in poetries and stories. He has recently authored the e-novel "it happened in delhi" and is working on few more. Besides, He has been actively participating on events those lead him to his passion. His works can be witnessed by his insta id- @thevaibhav_gupta

My hero

Sar pe dunia ka bojh liye,
Aankhon me kal ki chinta,
Par honthon pe fir bhi muskaan ko dekha hai..

Maine mere papa ke roop me,
Is duniya me bhagwan dekha hai ..

Jiske saye me maine.
Sardiyon ki dhoop se leke,
Sham ki chhaanv ko dekha hai..

Sach kahta hoon main,
Maine mere papa ke roop me,
Is dunia me bhagwan dekha hai ..

Apni khwashishon ko bhulake,
Hamare sapno mein jisne,
Apna is jeevan ko sameta hai..

Ha maine us pita mein mera,
Sach mein bhagwan dekha hai..

Yun to aksar hi ruth jate hai bachhe,
Gussa hoke kisi baat par,
Par bina khana khilaye na sone dene wale bhagwan ko,
Maine sach me dharti pe dekha hai..

Yun to aksar hi bhatak jata hoon main,
Kal ke bare mein sochkar.
Meri aankhon se dar ko door bhagate,
Maine aksar unko dekha hai..

Yun hi nahi main kahta hoon,
Maine mere papa ke roop mein,

Is dunia mein bhagwan dekha hai ..

Khwahishein aksar aasmaan chooti,
Par paanv zameen par rakhne ki kalaa ko dekha hai..
Maine mushkil halaaton me bhi,
Sabra ko taakat banaate dekha hai..

Ha mere papa ke roop mein,
Is dunia mein bhagwan dekha hai ..

Alfaazon se nahi ki bayaan ,
Par jisne apne karmon se pyar beshumar diya hai.
Main kaise kahu mere bhagwan maine,
Tumhare ansh ko dharti mein paa liya hai…

Ha mere papa ke roop mein,
Is dunia mein bhagwan dekha hai...

Devendra Dhakad

I am a student and a fresh content writer. Neither did a course of content writing nor written in any book before this one. My superheros are my parents. I'm in search of more stuff like this. If you guys want to hire me as a writer, dm me pls...

You can reach me by
Email- seetakishoredevendra@gmail.com
Instagram handle- devendra___dhakad & broken__heart_

पापा

मां के ऊपर तो सभी लिखते हैं,
 पर जिसके प्यार की कभी कोई बात नहीं की जाती, वो हैं पापा|
पूरा परिवार यूं ही एक साथ नहीं चलता,
इस अनदेखी डोर को जिसने है संभाला वो हैं पापा| जिनकी खुद की जिंदगी ब्लैक एंड व्हाइट है,
पर मेरी जिंदगी में खुशियों के रंग भरे, वो हैं पापा| हजारों दर्द सीने में छुपाए बैठे हैं वो,
 पर जिसने मेरी आंख में एक आंसू तक ना आने दिया, वो हैं पापा।
जिंदगी में जब पहली बार हार से रूबरू हुआ तो पूरी तरह टूट चुका था मैं,
पर जिसने आकर मुझे संभाला, वो हैं पापा|
हर मोड़ पर मैंने सिर्फ और सिर्फ धोखा ही खाया है, पर हमेशा से जिसने मेरा साथ निभाया, वो हैं पापा| जब जब इस जालिम दुनिया ने मुझे डराया,
तब जिस सुपर हीरो ने आकर मुझे बचाया, वो हैं पापा|
जिंदगी के उस गहरे अंधेरे में बहुत ठोकरें खाईं मैंने,
पर आखिर में जिसने उम्मीदों का चिराग जलाया, वो थे पापा|
अपनी नादान हरकतों की वजह से जिस अनमोल रत्न को मैंने अपने हाथों से खो दिया और मुझे एहसास तक ना हुआ, वो थे पापा|
पूरी जिंदगी वह फरिश्ते की तरह मेरी तकलीफें कम करने की कोशिश करते रहे,
 पर मैं नालायक जिसे ना समझ पाया, वो थे पापा| जिसने हमेशा मेरी भलाई की फ़िक्र की,
और मैं ताउम्र उन्हें गलत समझता रहा वो थे पापा| मैं आज इस मुकाम पर खड़ा हूं,
पर जो इसके असली हकदार थे वो थे मेरे पापा |अब जाकर समझा तो उन्हें बहुत याद करता हूं, समय रहते जिसे ना समझ पाया वह थे पापा| कहने को वह आज मेरे पास सब कुछ है,
मगर जिस शख्स के प्यार की कमी है हां वही है मेरे पापा.....

Ashis Pahi

Ashis Pahi, pursuing Master Degree in Commerce, and regular writer in YourQuote platform since 2017. He loves to write poems, shayari, quotes, and spares his time in reading novels and try to learn different languages. He strongly believe in himself.

IG: @ashis_luku95

Hero of my Life

Literally, no one in the universe can write or describe his father in some words or in some lines. Father, Dad, Papa all means a lot and indicates to one person and, we represent in different forms. A father who becomes a hero stands in all situations to protect his family and children if they are in a big problem and going to face any. I'm going to talk about every father who is a hero for everyone but we don't try to understand him according to our own age. In the different stages of our life, we treat him differently. At the age of college life, we don't prefer to listen to our parent's words later on, after having maturity, we understand the reality of why our father opposes us?

In Hindu mythology, it has cleared mentioned that the son grows up and reaches 18 years father treats him like a friend and starts to share everything.

It was 22nd September 1961 he came to this world and create himself gone to college for graduation in 1978-81 and after the college life he got his first posting in 1984 in a Primary school as an English teacher and after 1 year left the job. In 1988 he got another job in Govt Irrigation Dept as Jr. Clerk and later he achieves promotions in his life. It was 1995 after I'm blessed to come into this beautiful world. I'm now 25 being younger than my sister and brother has done a lot of mistakes knowingly and unknowingly, being my father's loveable one so never beaten rather scolded.

It's my own thought my father and mother are my two eyes and I can see because of them.

Being my father is too strict, punctual, and straightforward so much in his life feeling blessed I have those qualities in me. A father so as his son. Your own character and image reflect the image of your father inside you.

Father has taught me one thing "try to respect girls and first make a relation with a girl as your sister if you keep that

relation then you can go for another girl with whom you want to spend your entire life."
Being sorry I couldn't fulfill my father's dream what he wants to make me.
Still, he is with me and supporting me. Thank you.

Smita Kumari

She is a student
And writer by passion.
She loves to read and write.

IG: @mk.singh3330

मेरे पापा

वह जो बड़ी-बड़ी मुश्किलो को,
पल में सुलझा देते हें।
वो जो परेशानिया को मुझ तक,
आने से पहले हिं लोटा देते हे।

मेरे खुशियों मे मेरे साथ,
हर मुश्किलो मे थामे मेरा हाथ।
नायक हे जो मेरे,
पापा हे वो मेरे।

मेरे सफलता पर बधाई,
हार पर दिलासा,
हमेसा देते हें,
मुझे कुछ नया कर दिखाने की आस।

दुआ लगे उन्हे अल्लाह की,
मिले उन्हे हर खुशियाँ जीवन की।
उनके बुढापे का सहरा रहूंगी,
आँखों का तारा रहूंगी।

Ankita Sahoo

Hello this is Ankita .Well I'm an introvert and a bookworm as well, extremely passionate about penning my thoughts. Want to serve my nation being an IAS officer.

(1)

The Father is not only a person, he is the pillar of a family. The backbone, the supporting hand in a family. We always look after him as our role model, as an ideal; whose appearence is more than enough to give that postive energy to face all the obstacles on the way. In TV we see the reel heroes but in real life my real and all time favourite hero is my "DAD". He is that gift from God which every child would wish to get as his/her father. He never asks for anything for himself rather fulfils all the unasked wishes of ours. He is my superhero. I am blessed to have him as my father and I want to make him feel proud of his daughter .No word in the world would be enough to thank him for his deeds, his immense love, care, affection still I just want to say Thank You Papa for being who you are. And I love you Dad.

(2)

Dad at times can be the strictest person but yet can be the sweetest friend, who is ever ready to solve all the problems faced by his children. Today's generation is tending to neglect their parents but they should know the value of that priceless and most expensive gift that they have received from God without asking for it. Every father is a gem in disguise .His guidance leads us to the path of success and immense happiness. This is the least I could write on my part for my DAD and to all the Father's out there. This one's a small tribute to the backbone of each and every family.

निरज यादव

निरज यादव का जन्म 1 जनवरी, 2005 में बिहार के मोतिहारी जिले के नयकाटोला गाँव मे हुआ था। उनकी कुछ कविताएँ 'अमर उज्जाला' अखबार मे छपी है। उनकी एक कविता को चेतना नामक मासिक पत्रिका मे स्थान दी गई है। हाल ही मे उन्होंने अपनी एक कविता संग्रह पुस्तक प्रकाशित की है। उनके पुस्तक का नाम है , "कविताएँ कोरोना काल की"।

IG: @authornirajyadav

पापा, आप ही हो सबसे महान

क्यों मुझे बिठाये हो छाँव में?
जबकि छाले पड़े है आपके पाँव में
आपने इतना मुझे क्यों दिया है सुख?
कि झेलना पड़ा आपको दुख।
पापा, आपने हर मेरी ख्वाहिशों को पूरा किया।
अपनी ख्वाहिशों को आपने क्यों अधूरा किया?
अपने - आपको गिराकर, मुझे सिखाया जिंदगी का उड़ान,
पापा, आप ही हो सबसे महान।
आपने ऊँगली पकड़कर चलाना सिखाया है,
अपने ही तो मुझे सही राह दिखाया है ।
मैं प्रयत्न करूँगा कि दे सकुँ जीवन भर सम्मान,
पापा, आप ही हो सबसे महान।
पापा, से ही मेरा जीवन पूरा होता है,
पापा ना हो तो परिवार अधूरा होता है।
पापा आप है तो समाज मे मेरा भी होता है सम्मान,
पापा, आप ही हो सबसे महान।

Kalamkaar

This is Kalamkaar. He is from Uttrakhand bought up in Meerut (UP). His hobbies are reading and writing. His interest is in writing. He loves writing. He is part of 295+ Anthologies as Co-Author. He won 290+ Certificate in Writing, He Start writing 29 February 2020. He is part of 4 anthology as Co Author going for record and he is omg record holder as Co -Author of Book Called Laposia. He is part of 6 international Anthologies as Co-Author. He is simple and people observer. His insta handle is kalamkaar51 and email is kalamkaar51@gmail.com. He believes in Karma.

पिता को समर्पित कविता

सोचे ना ख़ुद के बारे मे पहले
ढाल बनकर ख़ुद परिवार मे आयी परेशानियों से ख़ुद लड़ जाते है।
सँभालते है परिवार को हर हालत मे
भूके रहकर ख़ुद दिल के टुकड़ो को पहले वो खिलाते है।
खरीदते ख़ुद के लिए कुछ नहीं मगर अपने बच्चो को सब कुछ दिलाते है।
बूरे हालातो मे भी बच्चो की ज़िद्द पूरी करते जाते है
परेशानिया ख़ुद पर लेने से नहीं घबराते हैं।
न्योछावर करदे ख़ुद को परिवार के लिए है
करते ख़ुद के लिए कुछ नहीं, परिवार की बिगड़ी परिस्थिति को सँभालते है।
पहनते नहीं वो ख़ुद चाहें कपडे अच्छे, मगर बच्चो को अपने सबसे अच्छे कपडे पहनते है।
रखते ध्यान नहीं ख़ुदका, परिवार का ध्यान खुदसे पहले रखते है।
मेहनत करते ख़ुद इतनी के चेहरे पर सिकन नहीं आने देते, बनो बच्चो तुम अफसर उनसे ये है कहते है।
हो जाये अगर बच्चे दूर तो उस गमको वो अकेले सहते, किसी और से नहीं कहते है।
बच्चो की ख़ुशी के लिए सब कुछ अपना खो देते है
अपनों बच्चो के आंखों मे अस्सू नहीं देख सकते है, उनके गम भी ख़ुद सहते है।
पिता इनको कहते है

Jeevitha.S

She is a girl with stupendous writing skills. Her heart is a castle abound with unbreakable courage, being contained with enticing dreams. Penning is her way of spreading aesthetic vibes among her readers. Being a literarian is her pride. She loves to be a unicorn amidst the flock of sheep's!

My Eminent Man

The super hero who never failed on his duties,
The one who made my life more enticing,
He gave me all that he had,
He created a world full of invocations for me,
Nothing is precious than his love for me,
He made me into a enthralling princess,
His presence could make my pain evanesce,
His love for me is unruly,
He illuminated me with much freedom,
His trust on me is the best invocation in my life,
He is the one behind my vibrance,
He is my contentment,
The eminent man in my life, my dad...

Harshita Verma

Co-author Harshita Verma is a good writer from Lucknow. She has completed her graduation in commerce stream. She has been writing poetry for 6 months as her passion. She wants to be a novelist in future.
IG: @0__hsh

MY SUPERHERO- MY FATHER

My dad my superhero
You do not always show yours emotions but I know I am your world
You do not always tell about your wishes but I will fulfill them
You are not only my father but my everything.

My dad my superhero
You are always there at times of need
You are always there for advices
You are always there when I am alone
You are not only my father but also my friend.

My dad my superhero
Though we do not talk much you always understand me.
Though you are sometimes strict but I know it is for my benefit.
Many things can change but you will always be my superhero.

MY DAD

My dad working for the welfare of his family.
Spending his days and night in fulfilling the dreams of family.
Sacrificing his leisure but never saying anything.
Always prioritising the needs of family before his needs.
If not him then who is a hero.

My dad managing to play with me on weekends.
Even though he needs to rest still he has time for me.
Always ready to solve any problem I face during any stage of life.
If not him then who is a hero.

शुभाशीष रंजन

शुभाशीष रंजन जमालपुर {बिहार} से एक बेहतरीन कवि हैं। उन्हें SR36 के एक पेन नाम के साथ रोमांटिक और प्रेरक कविताएं / उद्धरण लिखने का शौक है।आप उनकी इंस्टाग्राम आई.डी. @ranjanshubhashishish और YourQuote आई.डी. Shubhashish Ranjan पर जाकर उनकी कविताओं/उद्धरण का एक मजा ले सकते हैं। शुभाशीष रंजन आपकी मांग पर भी कविताएं/उद्धरण लिख सकते है|

E-Mail:shubhashishishranjan36@gmail.com

प्यारे पापा

पापा ओ, मेरे प्यारे पापा,
हमारी खुशियों के लिए तोह आपने सबकुछ किया!
पर आज तक कभी बताया नहीं कि,
आपने फेस्टिवल्स पर नए कपडे क्यों नही लिया?
हमारे पूछने पर कुछ न कुछ,
बोलकर टाल दिया करते थे,
क्या आप अब बता सकते आपको क्यूँ,
आपके पुराने कपडे नए ही मालूम पड़ते थे?
अच्छा लगता जैसे आप मेरी
गुणगान सबको किये फिरते है
गलती से भी,कोई मेरे खिलाफ बोले,
तो जिंदगी भर उससे चिढ़ते है¡
मम्मी को साथ मिलकर चिढ़ाना,
एक दूसरे को अपनी सीक्रेट्स बताना,
ये सब कभी आपने ही तो सिखाया है,
जब भी कभी कंफ्यूज रहा,
तो आपने ही तो रास्ता दिखाया है|
आपकी सिखायी हर एक बात,
जिंदगी भर न भूल पाउँगा,
खुशकिस्मत समझूंगा खुद को,
अगर अगले जन्म में भी आपको ही पाउँगा..

Krishna Motwani

Krishna Motwani is a Student currently.
She use to pen down her feelings.
She is a moody girl.
She started writing in the month of june,2020.
She writes in her free time.
She writes some motivational quotes or poetries too and practices artworks also.
She lives her life like a bird
As bird flies freely and enjoys life like that she also lives her life freely and enjoy fullest.
For motivating and inspiring poems and quotes, you can check her on IG: @ unique__blog_

पिता से है नाम मेरा!

पिता से है नाम मेरा,
बिना उनके मेरी जिंदगी में है अंधेरा।

करते हो दिन रात मेहनत हमारे लिए,
जानती हूँ मैं, आप कभी भी अपने दुख का इज़हार नहीं करते, हमारे खुशी के लिए।

मेरे सब नखरे सह लेते हो,
मेरी खुशी में खुद खुश रह लेते हो।

कभी हिम्मत हार जाती हूँ,
आपके बीत्तर मेरे लिए विश्वास देखकर फिर उठ जाती हूँ।

आपको छुप छुप कर रोते देखा है मैने,
खुद कब हिम्मत हार जाते हो पर मुझे पूरा हौसला दिया है आपने।

Padma Srivastava

Padma Srivastava, a poetess of mind and heart, born and brought up in Varanasi and started writing from her childhood. She became graduated from Banaras Hindu University with it she is also a good writer and singer. Now she is doing pg in Archaeology from Banaras Hindu University with it she has also been co _author of several anthologies till now. She is a book lover with it she is also a nature lover who spends her most of times with nature.
IG: _s_unknown_feelings

हमारे हीरो: हमारे पापा

अफसोस होता है
हां अफसोस होता है मुझे ये जानकर
दुख होता है मुझको ये सोचकर
ज़िन्दगी भर अपनी खुशियां लुटाकर हमें
खुशियां देता है कौन
और हम खुशियां लुटाते हैं किसपे
जीवन भर अपना जीवन हमपे लुटाता है कौन
और हम जीवन लुटाने को तैयार किसपे रहते हैं
जीवन की हर उलझनों से लड़कर
ज़िन्दगी की हर चोट को सहकर
जो कभी न मुस्कुराना छोड़े
जो लिखा भी न हो हमारी किस्मत में
उसको भी लाकर तकदीर में जोड़े
ऐसा शूरवीर भला हो सकता है कौन
हर फ़रमाइशों को कर दे झट से पूरा
ख़ुद के शौक का कोई ध्यान ही नहीं
बच्चे मेरे हर ख़ुशी पाए
अपने कोई अरमान ही नहीं
भला हमारा इतना ख़्याल रख सकता है कौन
छोड़ो ना इतना घूमाना भी क्या
स्वयं देवता भी झुके जिसके आगे
स्वयं दिशाएं भी जिसके प्रेम का प्रमाण हैं
जिसने किए हो इतने त्याग
भला उसके प्रेम से कौन अन्जान है
हर बच्चे का सपना, हर बेटी के ख़्वाब जो हो
उसके अलावा क्या चाहिये भी
जब सर पर हाथ पापा का हो
अपनी रातों की नींद उड़ भी जाए तो क्या

हमें चैन के जीवन की सैर कराएं
हमें तो हर कुछ चाहिए पसन्द की
भले वो ख़ुद भूखे रह जाएं
ख़ुदा आशिक दे या ना दे भले
पर पिता का साया हर बच्चे के नसीब में आए
नवाजे कुदरत हर बच्चे को खुशियों से
ज़िन्दगी भर के साथी जब पिता बन जाए
दे दे कुर्बानियां अपने खुशियों की
ऐसा कोई कर सकता है क्या??
पिता तो कर सकता है हर कमियों को दूर
पर क्या कोई
पिता की कमी को दूर कर सकता है क्या??

Hema Kirthiga J.

She is Hema Kirthiga J, and her pen name is sparkle. She is professionally a psychologist and passionately a writer. She heals others but writing heals her. She is writer, reader, orator and a believer. She is from Chennai. She lives by the principal of inspire and be inspired. She writes her heart and soul and she deeply believes that the depth of her heart and the nib of her pen are soulfully connected. Writing is an art and she is a proud artist. She loves what she does and loves what she writes. You can reach her at

Instagram- @the_pen_queen
Email- inker.sparkle@gmail.com
Yourquote – JKM

WHO IS HE?

He is my friend,
He is my love,
He is my sweet heart,
He is my co player,
He is my artist,
He is my muse,
He is my teacher,
He is my guide,
He is my care taker,
He is my love shower,
He is my blessing,
He is my child,
He is my study partner,
He is my soul mate,
He is my creative thinker,
He is my idea giver,
He is my advisor,
He is my lucky charm,
He is my super human,
He is my wonderful man,
He is my best,
He is my sweetest,
He is,
None other than my dad.

Jayashree Sahoo

Jayashree Sahoo is habitant of ODISHA.

Her writings started on yourquote, notojo and mirakee like writing platforms. You can search her on yourquote by name of Jaya Jayashree. Nowadays she is member of many writing communities and earned a alots of certificates through her writings.

She is Co.author of 160+ anthologies .Also she is Compiler of many anthologies in Hindi, English and Odia languages. Currently she is working as project head and board member of a reputed publication.

According to her, if you dont express your inner feelings towards someone, then just write those on a paper and making yourself happy for without reason.

Insta id -@mixing_of_emotions
Email.id- jayashreesahoo665@gmail.com

FATHER IS WORLD

.

Dear my papa,
I love you more than me in without reason,
You are one in all for me,
If there give award to best father,
Then you win that award must, as my bestest father,
Papa is not just a word for calling,
Its my happiness and my emotion for expressing,
How much you important to me,
I can't describe in just words
How much I love you,
I can't express in just saying,
You dont encourage for achieve goal,
But you saying always having selfbelieve and hard work making you winner,
Thats just words are very important in my path of life for making me better,
Your guidance, your love, your care, your affection and your sacrifice ,
Always in my bottom of heart, which gives me hope for making you proud once,
I know, you hide too many woes in front of me and learn new,
But I understand papa, you want to make strong as you.

Shivani Singh

Name - Shivani Singh
Father's Name - Mr.Dhirendra Pratap Singh
Mother's Name - Mrs. Kavita Singh.

"पिता"

बिना उसके ना एक पल भी गंवारा है
पिता ही साथी है, पिता ही सहारा है।

मेरे अजीज हो आप,
मेरे सबसे अच्छे दोस्त हो आप
हर इच्छा पूरी करने वाले,
खुदा से बढ़कर हो पापा आप।

ज़िन्दगी जीने का मज़ा तो आपसे मांगे हुए सिक्कों से था,,
"पापा"
हमारी कमाई से तो ज़रूरतें भी पूरी नहीं होती....

किसी ने पूछा : वो कौन सी जगह है जहाँ हर ग़लती ,
हर जुर्म और हर गुनाह माफ़ हो जाता है ?
मैंने मुस्कुराते हुऐ कहा, मेरे पापा का दिल

"पिता"
एक स्तंभ हो आप,
एक विश्वास हो आप,
आपसे है अस्तित्व मेरा,
पिता ये नाम हो आप ।...

कंधो पर झुलाया, प्यार से कंधो पर घुमाया।।
पापा की बदौलत ही मेरा जीवन खुबसूरत बन पाया।।

ये जो मुस्कान लिए बैठें हैं
पिताजी की ,
पहचान लिए बैठें हैं ।

Devyani Neral

She is a co-author of 50 anthologies and a published poet. 24 years of her age has given her innumerable thoughts to write. She is an engineer by profession and a writer by passion.Reading thrills her and feels her with joy and so does writing. She is currently writing her first book which will be of self - help genre. Motivational writings are her cup of tea. She strongly believe that we are here to write our own story and create our own path.
IG: @neraldevyani

The unconditional love of Father.

He created me, He raised me .
Whatever is the situation, he always praised me.

My achievement gets double when he smiles.
My life becomes worthy when he wears that pride.

He accepts my success and call himself a proud father.
He accepts my flaws and give me life lessons.

He bears that pain silently
And heal those wounds quietly.

I owe my life to him,
Because he is the one who gave me wings.

Drishti Bai

Fun loving
Ready for thrill
Karma believer
Future psychologist
Writer at instagram @heart_diaries07

Papa bolo ya superhero baat toh ek hi hai. Aisa insaan jo apni khusiya chorke humre khushiya pure krta hai wo super hero se kam toh nahi ho skta
Maa toh 9 mahine pet mei rakhte hai lekin papa pure zindage dil mei.

Betiyo ke phele hero hote hai unke papa maano jese bas wahi unke sab kuch hai. Zindage ko jeena seekhate hai wo, sab pareshaniya hatake muskarate hai wo .
Aise hi kahani hai mre aur mere papa ki gusse mei dono ka ek samaan maano parchhai hu mei unki lekin pyaare hai wo mujhe sab se. Agar papa aur mere larie hojye toh maano khushiya hi gayab ho jate hai zindage se. Mere papa toh koi sahi baat bhi etne gusse se bolte hai ki jese galat hi lgne lag jate hai.

Abhi mere umar zyda nhi lekin unke pareshani dekhkar dil baith sa jata hai. Mei apne papa ki pure carbon copy hu jese wo sochte hai wese mei bhi wo alag baat hai ki generation gape ke karan kuch kuch chize nahi milti.
Jis tarah wo dusro ke liye sochte hai aur krte hai mei bhi kuch aise hi hu
Yeh dusro ki maddat krne ki adat hume dadaji se aaye hai.

Life kitne mushkil hote agar bhagwan yeh pita naam ka ensaan na deta . Ese dekhwate duniya mei pita hi toh hai jo hamre liye sochta hai. Hume roshni dekhar khud jalta hai bilkul suraj ki tarah.

Baap ameer ho ya garib wo apni aulad ke liye koi kami nahi chorta. Wo toh pure duniya se ladh jata hai.
Lekin aaj ki generation apne maa baap ki kadar nahi kar paate kyuki hum dekhwe mei etne ghum hogya h ki hume pta hi nhi hamare kon hai or kon paraya
Lekin dosto, hazro log ayge aur hazaro log jyge ek baap hi hai jo kabhi saath nahi chorta. Agar tum bade horhe ho toh wo bhi budhe horhe hai esliye unki kadar kro aur unke sth samay bitao kyuki waqt puchkar nahi ata

Bilal Khan

#मन कीं बात

Yes I'm an introvert. No I'm not shy. No I'm not stuckup. No I'm not antisocial. I'm just listening. I'm just observing. I can't stand small talk but can talk about life for hours.

Email ID: bilal9694khan@gmail.com

मेरी इज्जत मेरी शोहरत मेरा रुतबा मेरा मान है "पिता"
मुझको हिम्मत देने वाला मेरा अभिमान है "पिता".....

मेरा पिता मेरा अभिमान

कभी अभिमान तो कभी स्वाभिमान है पिता
कभी धरती तो कभी आसमान है पिता
जन्म दिया है अगर माँ ने
जानेगा जिससे जग वो पहचान है पिता...."
"कभी कंधे पे बिठाकर मेला दिखता है पिता...
कभी बनके घोड़ा घुमाता है पिता...
माँ अगर मैरों पे चलना सिखाती है...
तो पैरों पे खड़ा होना सिखाता है पिता....."
"कभी रोटी तो कभी पानी है पिता...
कभी बुढ़ापा तो कभी जवानी है पिता...
माँ अगर है मासूम सी लोरी...
तो कभी ना भूल पाऊंगा वो कहानी है पिता...."
"कभी हंसी तो कभी अनुशासन है पिता...
कभी मौन तो कभी भाषण है पिता...
माँ अगर घर में रसोई है...
तो चलता है जिससे घर वो राशन है पिता...."
"कभी ख़्वाब को पूरी करने की जिम्मेदारी है पिता...
कभी आंसुओं में छिपी लाचारी है पिता...
माँ गर बेच सकती है जरुरत पे गहने...
तो जो अपने को बेच दे वो व्यापारी है पिता...."
"कभी हंसी और खुशी का मेला है पिता...
कभी कितना तन्हा और अकेला है पिता...
माँ तो कह देती है अपने दिल की बात...
सब कुछ समेत के आसमान सा फैला है एक जहान हैं पिता...
उन के होने से बख़्त होते हैं...
बाप घर के दरख़्त होते हैं...

Sayak Ghosh

The guy with the rock-solid presence in his child's life, the one who shepherds his child in the right direction with a firm but loving hand, the one every child absolutely relies on needs to be celebrated everyday! As such, when it comes to parenting, mothers seem to take the cake and are showered with appreciation. But behind every successful mom is the silent and strong presence of a father. He might not be celebrated as much as a mother, but his contribution to the family and the welfare of his children should be acknowledged. It is time that every child says that "my dad is my hero".

IG: @sayak_ghosh31

1. Dad teaches them discipline

While a mother coddles and protects her child, a father disciplines her. More often than not, he teaches his child right from wrong. He is the moral compass with which the child learns to navigate the choppy waters of life.

2. A father leads by example

A child always picks up work ethics from his father. When he sees his father helping with chores at home, he does the same. A father who is efficient at office work inspires his child to be a thorough professional as well. A father who is able to maintain a good work-life balance is an ideal role model for his child.

3. Daddy teaches from his child's mistakes

A father teaches his child that failure is not the end of life. He shares the lessons he has learnt from failure with his child so that he can avoid making the same mistakes.

4. Papa is reliable

Even though he may have a meeting with a client or an important presentation to make, a good father will always make time for his children. A father who is there for his children when they need him is reliable and hence will always have his children's trust.

5. Dad never gives up on you

A father is the best cheerleader for his child. Even though he may be tough on them, he has their best interest at heart. He will always cheer them on and encourage them to be the best they can.

6. Daddy is a problem solver

Fathers listen to problems and will do whatever is in their power to get their children out of trouble. The child may get

sounded off later, but when it matters the most, the father will always be there for his child, ready with a solution.

7. A father is a trusted advisor
Fathers are the best advisers. Be it something as minor as a school project or something as life-altering as which college course to choose from, a father's input can make all the difference. A papa is reliable.

8. Dad is a tough taskmaster
Fathers do not mince words when it comes to their child's well-being. Usually, a father wants his child to come out on top of everything she does And, the only way to do that is to be critical of her work. His criticism is positive and constructive and will mould the child well.

9. A father is fun
Though a father is assigned with the tough task of being the disciplinarian of the family, he is also fun to be around. He knows when to take a break and relax with his child. Be it playing a game of cricket or sitting down for an imaginary tea party with all the dolls in the house, a father knows how to engage his child and nurture her fun side.

Udayan Chetia

Udayan Chetia was born on September 26, 2003 to a middle class family of Dhemaji district, Assam. He is also known by his nickname "Ron". He started writting poems, quotes, short-stories etc; when he was in 6th standard in English, Hindi and Assamese languages. Udayan pursued his HSLC Exam from Vivekananda Kendra Vidyalaya, Dhemaji in the year 2019 and currently studying at Crescent Academy, Jorhat. His most of the writings were published on his school magazine "Jnanam". He was inspired by his father for writing as his father himself is a writer.
IG: @udayanc_official

The Father

The father is the one
who catch you before
you fall.

The father is the one
who tries to keep you
smile.

The father is the one
who doesn't shows
his pains to you
and keep you far from
making mistakes.

The father is the one
who want nothing
from you, and
loves you when you cry,
scolds you when you
make mistakes.

Kareena Verma

She is a computer science student and co-author of many Anthologies and just like her name Kareena delineate alike her name , sanguine with her soul, pure with her heart , innocent with her straightforward thoughtful perceptions!
For her Rectitude within her is everything & nothing is above than Viracity with our nation , she wants only to flame alike terracotta Diya, for one day she'll spread the happiness of lights as the most bright star in the sky of someone home and wanna to spread love of humanity every where!
IG: @Warrior_thephoenix_birdie

Dad the whole world of a Home

The world, the soul of a Home,
Without you we can't consider our
Life, you are the roof of our life,
Sometimes you become my friend
The best ever person who understands me only
Sometimes you become my best solution box in my every problems of
My life,
Sometimes you become my super hero
Of my life,
Thankyou papa for your every sacrificed for me, that you give me a better life everytime to secrificed your own dreams! I can't explain your love with words ever!
But I hurt a lot when you never be take care of yourself, those wonderful hands during Working, those pain that you never share with us,
please I'm here papa Love always!

Dear Papa,

You never be know about my love for you ever, that's really true, the Communication distance make so
much distance between both of us,
I can't able to express my feeling's
front of ever, you always think I'm very
Stubborn, egostic girl, a silly girl who never be understand her
responsibility always chatting with her friends and misusing her freedom , but today I wanna tell you that
trust me papa!
I never become like that girl , who will hurt you, I always fallow your valuable morality in my life, I always do Hardworking like you papa!
Trust me papa! One day sure I'll make you so much proud of you to myself!
I promise you, and maa-papa I can't live without you both ever!

Debesh Prusty

Debesh lays his foundation for writing in books as a co-author from his graduation time. It is never too easy for him to overcome the difficulties. He used to write from that day when everyone called him an overthinker. He just loved to write microtales than other genres. Hope everyone will love to read his writings. He is too moody, writing is his constant though.

Email id: prustydebesh@gmail.com
Instagram handle @Trapatale

Some sacrifices are inestimable

Of all the titles of relationship I have, Father has always be the best. Father is the person of the family who sacrificed everything. He is an ideal person of everyone's life. Father is the person who handles every hard situation of our family. God has no faces, but for every child father is just like God. Noone can give that love and caring except father in this world.

May be he looks hard from outside but he is soft from inside just like a coconut. He is like a tree , he burns himself with problems but always keep his family under shadows of himself. He confronts every bad times boldly but never shows that to anyone.

May be he is not friendly like other members but he can understand his children very well. He works hard for us and always want to keep us happy. May be he has been wearing a pair of shoes from last 1 year but he never forgets to buy shoes for his children and his family members during any occasion or festival.

He sacrifices everything for his family. May be he is using a old keypad mobile but he never hesitates for buying costly phones for his children. After getting monthly salary he never buys anything for himself but he never forgets to buy something for his children and family members. His sacrifices are just inestimable.

Appreciate your father even if he don't give anything costly to you , finding him by your side everytime is the most worth for you. We can't never feel what he went through for his children and family members. His goodness is higher than the mountain and depper than the sea.

If love is the symbol of mother
Then sacrifice is the symbol of father
Don't underestimate the word Father
Not everyone have father
You should feel happy that you have him.

Pragyan Panda

Pragyan is persuing her B.Tech in "Chemical Engineering" from IGIT, Sarang. She's a short girl from Rourkela, Odisha. With fascination of nature, she's a spiritual person who motivates people. She does weird stuff like interacting with non living ones and pens down her mind. For more of her works, do follow her IG @quote_love_97.

MY GUIDE: MY FATHER

How to describe the depth of ocean?
Measure the vast sky dimensions;
Adopt to the life with its lessons_
And ignore guilts with no attention.

Getting gifts as much he can afford:
The best guide and lifetime support;
The ultimate one to heal all pains_
The one who experienced summer when it rains.

As much as he can, he keeps on giving!
Until he finds us best in surviving_
He keeps on motivating throughout struggle:
Shows life's rules from every angle!!

Alas! His efforts are least appreciated;
We hardly realise his deficit after he's departed;
Even if we are earning and capable_
Reply if I'll get you point one percent of your deeds when I'm able!!

Priyanka Varma

She is Priyanka Varma studying Master's of Pharmacy from Visakhapatnam. She is a National and Central Zonal Sports Player along with being a Classical Dancer and an Artist. Along with these, she is also fond of writing her thoughts. She believes that "No-one in this world can love a girl more than her Father".
IG: @priyanka_varma_

DAD’S GIRL

Daddy,
You were one of the first I laid eyes on when I came into this world.
A little hand wrapped around a big finger With brown eyes looking up.
I didn't know you at first, but you were my daddy and later to become my hero.
You were one of the first I loved.
I chose you over my pink stuffed bear.
I loved how you'd pick me up and hug me; I'd feel so secure.
You'd lift me with one arm way above your head and play helicopter.
As I started to grow, you taught me to stand and walk.
You'd guide me so carefully so I wouldn't fall.
Once I began to walk on my own, you stood close by just in case I fell down.
If I did, you'd pick me up,
Wipe the tears off my face,
And a kiss for scrapped knee to be made all better
Once I got older, I didn't need your help walking, but I needed your love and time.
We'd play basketball; if I couldn't reach the basket, you'd lift me up so I could.
Making me feel like I was number one.
You'd do almost anything to see me happy.
A scared look to a reassuring face on the first day of school
The time Dad, you came back late from work after a long tiring day,
yet you went off to get my school supplies without cribbing.
Dad, every time I asked you for a certain amount of money,
you would give me more than what I asked for,
with that perfect smile of yours.
And a worried look to an excited girl on graduation day.

You always encourage me to try my best and support me one hundred and ten percent.
I've come to realize that I'm a lot like you.
You help me realize common sense isn't that common.
You also taught me to be witty.
You taught me how to deal with people and how to get what I want,
You taught me to raise my voice against the wrong.
And whenever someone says,
"You're just like your dad," I can't help but smile and be proud.
You're not only my dad, but you're also my hero.
Dad, even though I'm growing up, I still need your loving bear hugs,
And encouraging words of wisdom.
Don't forget I will always be your little baby girl,
And you will always be my loving father and hero.
I love you dad!
Daddy's Girl..!!

Nivetha R C

Nivetha R C, a young poetess from Coimbatore, Tamil Nadu. She graduated BA English Literature from PSGR Krishnammal College for Women. Currently, she is pursuing MA English in KSG College of Arts and Science, Coimbatore. She started writing poems from the age of 13. She used to write in Tamil and English.

Nivetha likes to personify the things around her and tries to reveal its emotions through her words.

She is interested to deliver the unheard conversations between two non-living things. She likes to write poems with rhyming words. Sometimes she uses to write acrostic poems too.

IG: @ahtevinchanmee

One Beautiful Soul

How can I imagine my life without my dad?
A day without him makes me get mad
It's difficult to believe how he laughs,
After a day full of work with tough
He is a simple man with basic accessory
But throughout my life, he provided with what is necessary,
Despite all works he hasn't avoided me
What kind of wonderful man is he?
One soul who shares his whole food
Never admits his bad mood
A man who loves me without many talks
Takes dresses only for family with a smile and walks
In my childhood, he was the one who taught me not to steal
The insults he faced for me it is difficult to heal
He even lived many days without wealth
But never failed to take care of my health...
What kind of a man he is? He never thinks of his birthday
But never neglected to make my birthdays as a special day
Yes, he doesn't know how to send a mail
But not even once he showed his face of pale
How can I deny that he is my first male friend?
Till now my journey with him continuous without any end
"Dad, you are my first guide
Thanks for standing by my side"
To me, he is the best father
Whatever our relatives tell about him, I don't bother
To the world, he may look like zero
But to me, he is my real hero.

Prangya Paramita sahu

१९९९ साल अप्रैल माह २१ तारीख को पिता महेश्वर साहू माता प्रतिमा साहू की कोख में प्रज्ञा परमिता साहू ने जन्म लाभ क्या है । अधुना खोलीकोट स्वयं शासित महाविद्यालय ब्रह्मपुर , ओड़ीसा कि शिक्षक शिक्षा स्नातक विभाग की २ वर्ष की छात्री है । पढ़ाई के साथ साथ अभीनय करना ,एंकरिंग करना और तर्क में हिस्सा लेने के लिए पसंद है।

(1)

गुस्सा बहुत करते हैं फिर भी प्यार करते हैं,
नंगा पाव हो चलते हैं हमें गाड़ी देते हैं,
खुद कभी तारीफ करते नहीं ,दूसरे जब तारीफ करते हैं हो खुश होते हैं ,,
हो और कोई नहीं है हो मेरी पापा है हो मेरी पापा है ।।

पापा

पापा इन दो शब्दों सिर्फ सुनने में ही अच्छी नहीं लगती है साथ साथ इन दो शब्दों का महत्व हमारे जिंदगी में अनेक है। पापा ऐसी इंसान होती है जो हमारी एक कष्ट देख नहीं पाते हैं, जो खुद फटे हुए कपड़े पहनते हैं पर हमें अच्छे कपड़े पहनते है ।। जो खुद पैदल चलकर इधर उधर जाते हैं वह हमें स्कूटी दिलाते हैं। पापा तो वह होती है जिसके पैर में चप्पल नहीं होती पर हमारे लिए हजारों चप्पल के मल खोल देते हैं । पापा तो हो होती है जिसको दो वक्त की रोटी नहीं मिलती फिर भी वह हमारे लिए पिज़्ज़ा ऑर्डर कर लेते हैं। पापा तो हो होती है जो खुद पढ़ी नहीं होते हैं फिर भी हमें एक अफसर बनाने के लिए सपना देखते हैं अफसर बनाने के लिए कोशिश भी करते हैं। पापा तो वह होते हैं जो हमारी खुशियों में हमारे साथ रहते हैं और हमारे आंखों में एक बूंद आंसू आने के लिए नहीं देते हैं।

आज हम प्राची के पापा के बारे में जानते हैं जो एक सरल इंसान है जिसके मन में ना किसके लिए भेदभाव है ना कपट है। अपने बेटों बेटियों को बहुत लाड प्यार से बड़ा करते हैं। प्राची की परिवार में उसकी दादी मां दादाजी एक चाची और चाची की दो बेटियां हैं परिवार में सब के ख्यालों प्राची के पापा हैं रखते हैं खाना पीना सब कुछ, दादा दादी के लिए दवाई ,बच्चों की पढ़ाई की खर्चा सब देते हैं। इतने दुख में रहने के बाद भी प्राची कि पापा ने सबके साथ मिलते हैं प्राची के पापा तो परिवार की हीरो थे सब की पक्का वाला दोस्त थे । पापा तो पापा होती है हर वक्त में प्राची के साथ देती है ।

Mohanapriya.K

Co-author Mohanapriya.K is a good writer from Tamilnadu, India. She has completed her Bachelor's degree in Engineering. She has been a writer for one year as her passion. She wants to be a best compiler and curator in future. Yet she sincerely hope that this writing journey of her will bring her many successes. She also loves singing.

My one and only super hero is my dad

My dad is my super hero.
My dad has helped me to fulfill all my dreams in my life.
He is my best friend.
It is said that there is a woman behind every man's success.
As true as it is, there will always be a man behind every woman's success - and this is true!
Because the role that men play in a woman's life as a father, uncle, son, grandfather, brother, husband and friend is not small.
And the duties involved in these positions are not insignificant.
Men who never forget all such duties and perform them with the utmost affection hold an important and everlasting place in the lives of women.

My dad is my best friend

We celebrate more special days every year to honour such mens in our life.
Thus women who make a woman's life better by her actions and make women better in their lives are always admirable and special.
Men also have many worries in mind.
Even if they do not express them, there will still be mental anguish within them.
Men who value women as fellow human beings without seeing women as inferior to men are always superior.
The value that women give to men should depend on what they do.
His father is the super hero in the lives of many daughters.
So high are men in the lives of women.

Shradha Gindlani

Shradha Gindlani is from a small town with big dreams taking hold of her heart and brain, day and night. With a vision of community to serve those in need of education and literacy she aspires high. She writes poetries and prose mainly. She is kind hearted and helping personality indeed.
IG: @shradha_gindlani

क्योंकि

मेरे आँसू से वो हस्ती और आप रोते है
मेरी हँसी से वो उलझती और आप सुलझते है
मेरी ज़िद से वो कतराती और आप हँस पड़ते है
मेरी वो ग़ैर है और आप अपने
क्योंकि
ये दुनिया मजबूत है और मेरे पापा कमजोर

Shadma Ali

Shadma Ali is a graduate in Accounting and Finance Hons and is currently working in E&Y GDS. She did her schooling from Loreto and grads from GCCBA , Kolkata. She is a young writer who has a flair for writing.

Contact on : shadmaali2020@hotmail.com

My World

My dad has always been my inspiration. I have learnt many skills & virtues from him. The way he works so hard for the family. I have seen him but clothes for us on festivals and nothing for himself out of his own hard earned money.

Honesty is a virtue which I imbibed from him. Once we went to buy something from a shop. When we almost returned home, we saw the shopkeeper had returned us more money that what we gave him. My dad went all the way back to return his money.

I have seen my father work day and night to earn for us and never keep a penny for himself. Every gift he receives he so lovingly shares with us.

He is my rock of Gibraltar who protects me always and his eyes fill with tears if anything befalls me. No amount of words will ever be enough to appreciate or talk about papa.

Ankita Bhatia

A Delhi based simple 20 years old girl pursuing B.Sc and completed with Diploma in travel and tourism management.
A special educator trainee and a tutor and now an Immigration Consultant as well by profession.
Ground Volunteer at Raindrops foundation helping people from backward section
Parents are her life their happiness is her strength.
Co author of 10+ anthologies and compiler of 5+ anthologies.
Writer on Instagram @_purposeoflife_by_ankita And entrepreneur @_ankita_encourage_talent And @shahanshahpublications on Instagram..Ex Content writer intern at 2 organizations.

Dad my hero my friend

Dad my hero my friend
The only one along with mom who will support me till the end.
Dad every daughter's first love
Dad who Never ditches her daughter
Who work hard to make his family feel comfortable
Every dad is a superhero
Every dad is special
None can replace him
None can share him except his daughter.

Papa aapki pari badi ho gayi
Lekin aapko chodegi nahi kabhi
Aapki pari bdai ho gayi
Lekin humesha aapka saaya banegi
Log bhale hi kahe betiyan prai hoti hai
Par aapki ye pari humesha aapke or mumma ke sath hi rahegi.
Aapki nanhi pari kahi nahi jayegi aapko chorkar

Love you mumma papa,
Ankita Bhatia.

Flairs and Glairs, a platform by a student for the students. We are esteemed youth struggling to carve out our path for our future and we follow a basic mindset Since everyone is not born with all-round skills. Joining hands with people who are born to execute it with perfection is the best way to evolve. Self-Evolution is the need of the hour but, evolving as a community is what we strive for. The initiative as kickstarted by, Founder- Mr. Shubham Shah with the motive to utilize the skillset and talent of writing has now a team of 10+ people who are actively participating into newer forms of learning and discovering talents among youngsters. We Provide platform and services like Publishing opportunities, Open mics, Workshops, Hands-on training. Operating with Brand Name of Flairs and Glairs (Publication House), we offer the chance of elevating a passionate writer to an esteemed author With Brand name Teekhe Zasbaaat. We bring to you an opportunity to get accustomed with the Public Speaking and Presenting of Thoughts along with regular challenges to brush up your inking spirit. The newest initiative to extend our services we introduced in a new writing Platform- The Glittering Fables and Ink Over Tears.

We Choose to Fly Like A Falcon than to be a Leg Pulling Crab.

www.ingramcontent.com/pod-product-compliance
Ingram Content Group UK Ltd.
Pitfield, Milton Keynes, MK11 3LW, UK
UKHW022005190726
13853UKWH00004B/1737